DETECTIVE ZACK

Trapped in Darkmoor Manor

JERRY D. THOMAS

Book 9

Pacific Press Publishing Association
Nampa, Idaho
Oshawa, Ontario, Canada

Edited by Aileen Andres Sox
Designed by Dennis Ferree
Cover and inside art by Kim Justinen

Copyright © 1997 by
Pacific Press Publishing Association
Printed in the United States of America
All Rights Reserved

ISBN 0-8163-1394-6

97 98 99 00 01 • 5 4 3 2 1

Dedication

Everywhere I go, kids tell me about their teachers
who are reading Detective Zack and other books
to their classes.

To those teachers who still read aloud to their students:
Thank you!
Your dedication and commitment are building the road
on which all authors walk.
Your love of books and reading is contagious.
May it spread like wildfire!

Other books by
Jerry D. Thomas

Detective Zack series

Detective Zack and the Mystery on the Midway

Detective Zack and the Secret in the Storm

Detective Zack Danger at Dinosaur Camp

Detective Zack and the Missing Manger Mystery

Detective Zack and the Mystery at Thunder Mountain

Detective Zack and the Red Hat Mystery

Detective Zack and the Secret in the Sand

Detective Zack and the Secret of Noah's Flood

Detective Zack's Word Puzzle Safari

Shoebox Kids series

The Mysterious Treasure Map

The Case of the Secret Code

Jenny's Cat-napped Cat

Mystery of the Missing Combination

The Broken Dozen Mystery

The Wedding Dress Disaster

The Cat in the Cage and Other Great Stories for Kids

Contents

1   What Do They Speak in England?   7
2   Darkmoor Manor   15
3   Inspector Zack   25
4   Something Terrible   33
5   Inspector Brown's Bobbies   41
6   Magic Murphey's Cell   49
7   Scrambled Messages   59
8   Setting a Trap   69
9   Good Trap, Wrong Person   77
10   The Thousand-Year Test   87
11   Trapped in Darkmoor Manor   97
12   Click, Clack, Clunk   105
13   The Duke of Marbury   113

CHAPTER ONE

What Do They Speak in England?

When you're flying in a plane that's about seven miles above the Atlantic Ocean, the water looks really smooth and blue. For a long time, all you can see is water—there's no land in sight anywhere. But don't let it fool you. Somewhere out there, past the middle of the ocean, just about the time you can see land again, there's a big bump.

I know, because that's where I lost my pencil— and I almost lost my lunch.

I was just starting to write in my notebook when we hit it. Everything around me flew up— and so did I. But my seat belt stopped me. Across the aisle, a man who was taking a drink got orange juice all over his face.

I would have laughed, but I was trying not to see my lunch again. It sounded like a kid in the row in front of us got to see his. But before long, the plane was calm again and so was my stomach. "Mom, I can't find my pencil and notebook. Can you see where they went?"

She looked over her shoulder at the seats behind us and shook her head. Then she leaned forward and peeked over the seat in front of her. Suddenly, she got a funny look on her face.

"Do you see them, Mom? Are they up there?"

"If they are, Zack, I don't think you want them anymore."

Just then, the kid in that seat threw up again. I decided Mom was right. "Maybe I can find new ones in London."

Mom says we didn't really hit a bump, just some turbulence (tur-bue-lints). "Turbu-what?" I asked.

"Turbulence," she answered. "That means that the air is 'bumpy.' It happens when a plane moves from an area where the air is moving up to where the air is moving down. We didn't really bounce up—the plane dropped down."

I guess it did make my stomach feel like it does when an elevator or a roller coaster heads down really fast. I don't like that feeling either. Anyway, I gave up on writing anything down. But that was OK. Before we left on this trip, Dad gave me a new detective tool—a tape recorder. It's so small it fits right into my pocket and uses those tiny little tapes.

"This is what a lot of people use to make notes or reminders for themselves," Dad said. "I think it's just what you need when it's too dark to write or when you just don't have time."

So I'm recording these notes, and I'll write them down later—when I get a new notebook!

Right now, if you were listening to this tape instead of reading, you'd hear a loud voice talking from the speakers over my head.

"This is your captain. Sorry about that bump back there—it snuck up on all of us. Flight control in London is reporting smooth skies all the way in from here, so feel free to stand up and walk around the cabin one last time before we begin to land. But when you are in your seat, keep your seatbelts fastened—just in case we hit another bump."

"We must be getting close," Mom said.

I crammed my face against the little window and tried to see ahead of the plane. "I can see land up ahead," I told her. "And clouds."

DETECTIVE ZACK

I'm really lucky I got to go on this trip. When Mom was invited to some meetings over here, she was really excited. "I'll have a chance to see where my great-grandparents lived. My mother always told me they lived in an old castle."

Of course, everyone wanted to go with her. And her trip *was* during our spring break from school. But Dad had to work, and Alex wasn't old enough. Kayla had already planned on a school camping trip with her friends. I started packing.

"Slow down there, Zack," Dad said. "There are a lot of things to do before you guys need to be packed." One of the things he did was call some friends we made on our trip to the Bible lands—Stefanie Townsend's parents.

You remember Stef—she was with me and Achmed (Ock-med) when we were searching for clues in the Bible lands.* The Townsend's were happy Mom and I were coming and insisted they would meet us at the airport.

Then Stef wanted to talk to me. "Zack, hurry and get here. I need your help—something odd is going on at Darkmoor Manor."

She was kind of whispering, and I wasn't sure I had heard her right. "What? Darkmoor Manor?" I asked.

"I can't explain now," she said. "Just hurry."

What Do They Speak in England?

Right. Like there was anything I could do to get there sooner. But it did make me *want* to get there sooner. As soon as we walked into the airport, I heard someone call my name.

"Zack!" someone called. I looked around, and there was Stefanie with her parents. Stef stepped up and gave my mom a bunch of flowers and a kiss on the cheek. Luckily, all she gave me was a punch in the arm.

Mrs. Townsend smiled. "Welcome to London. You must be dying to get out of those clothes. Dear, do get her bag." Mr. Townsend already had Mom's bag, and he led the way.

"So, what is Darkmoor Manor?" I finally got to ask Stef. "And what's going on there?"

"Darkmoor Manor is a museum. Father owns it, so I get to go there a lot."

"Your father owns a museum?" Suddenly, I liked Mr. Townsend a lot. "What kind of museum?"

She waved her hand. "Oh, the usual kind—old things from the old days here in England."

I liked that. "You mean it has suits of armor, like knights wore? And swords and axes?"

Stefanie nodded. "Yeah, stuff like that. And old books and maps and papers signed by kings or queens and gold coins and jewels that belonged to famous people."

That reminded me of something else. "Does Darkmoor Manor have any Bibles?"

She shrugged. "Probably. Why?"

So I told her about another problem. "Last week, my family went to a museum that had a lot of old books. The museum guide showed us some that were filled with stories from Rome and Greece hundreds of years ago. So Alex, my little brother, asked, 'Are they true stories?'

"The guide said, 'Not like true stories from the news today. Each one was probably about a real person once. But every time it was repeated, that person got stronger and braver. By the time the story was written down, not much that really happened was left.'"

Stefanie understood. "So you're wondering, what if the Bible is like that too? But Zack, we were there. We saw the places where the stories happened."

"I know," I agreed. "We saw the valley where the Bible says David fought Goliath. But how do we know that a kid fought a giant-sized soldier there? Maybe it was just a normal sword fight and people added stuff every time they told it."

Now Stefanie looked worried too. "How do we know if we can believe the Bible stories?" She shook her head. "Now we have two mysteries to solve."

We found our luggage while Mr. Townsend went to get the car. But when he drove up to the curb, something seemed wrong. When he stopped and hopped out, it hit me. He was on the wrong side of the car—but so was the steering wheel!

"Let's just slip these bags into the boot," he said as he grabbed Mom's.

I looked around, but I didn't see any boots. Then Mr. Townsend opened the car trunk. "Oh, the trunk. I thought you said 'the boot.'"

Stefanie turned to look at me. "The trunk?"

Mr. Townsend answered. "Trunk is what Americans call a car boot," he said to Stefanie. "They do use the strangest words sometimes."

"What?" I was confused. "We aren't the ones using the strange words. We're speaking English. What language do you speak here?" They both stared at me. Then I remembered where I was. "I guess you're speaking English, too, aren't you?"

Stefanie laughed. "Of course, Zack. You're so funny."

We were headed out of the airport when I looked up just in time to see a car on the wrong side of the road, heading straight toward us! All I could do was point over Mr. Townsend's shoulder. "Hey, look out for that car!"

DETECTIVE ZACK

He looked and then laughed. "Does my driving make you a bit nervous, Zack? It might be better if it weren't for all the cat paw prints all over my windshield. Stefanie, why must that cat of yours walk on my car?"

Stefanie giggled. "She just wants to see if anyone is inside."

The truth is, her dad's driving was making me nervous. I decided that he couldn't see out at all. Why else would he be driving on the wrong side of the road!

"Well . . . uh, you're not on the right side of the road," I managed to say as the other car raced past.

"Exactly," Mr Townsend agreed. "We're on the left side."

"No, I mean . . . we're supposed to be on the right side of the road."

"Yes," he agreed again. "Good thing that we are on the right side."

But we weren't on the right side—we were on the left side. And a big truck was headed right at us. I had to do something—either leap over the seat and grab the steering wheel away from him or duck behind the seat.

I ducked.

*Detective Zack and the Red Hat Mystery

CHAPTER TWO

Darkmoor Manor

No one else moved. In fact, they didn't even notice me or the truck that only missed my side of the car by inches. Well, I guess Mr. Townsend did.

"That lorry was a little close. It nearly plowed us right over."

But while he was talking, I was thinking. *The truck went by my window. And I'm sitting behind Mr. Townsend, who was driving. On the wrong side of the car—I mean the right side, not the left.*

Then I remembered. In the United States, people drive on the right side of the road. In England, people drive on the left side. Mr. Townsend was right where he should be driving—on the left side.

DETECTIVE ZACK

"Father," Stefanie called from beside me, "this isn't the way home. Where are we going?"

"I thought our guests might like to stop in at Darkmoor Manor," he answered. "Just for a quick minute.

"Yes, they would! Right, Zack?" I could only nod. "Thank you, Father!" She turned back to me. "You're going to be just mad about Darkmoor."

I decided she meant that I would be happy. "Hey, Stef, you still haven't told me what's going on there."

"Right," she answered. "About three months ago, strange things started happening. Ms. Huffington—she's the manager—says that nearly every morning, things are moved around—a desk drawer left open, some of the old museum things knocked about or rearranged. Things like that." She lowered her voice to a whisper. "She's beginning to think it might be haunted."

But she didn't whisper quietly enough—her father heard. "Darkmoor Manor? Haunted? Stefanie, I think not."

Her mother joined in. "Please, dear. Let's not fill Zack's mind with such rubbish."

Stefanie folded her arms. "I know it's not haunted. But how do you explain those things?"

Her mother clucked her tongue. "Maybe the

dear woman is simply growing forgetful. It does happen when one gets older." Then she changed the subject, like mothers do. "Look, there's the clock tower."

The Big Ben clock tower was one of the things I wanted to see in London. Mom and I both stared. "Wow," I said. "Don't forget to take a picture, Mom." But by the time she got her camera out, we had driven into a light rainstorm. Big Ben disappeared.

"We'll be back," Mom promised.

With the sound of the rain and the windshield wipers, Stef and I could talk without everyone listening. "In all the times things have been moved around, has anything been stolen?" I asked.

She shook her head. "Nothing."

I shrugged. "Maybe someone who stayed late or came in early moved those things. It doesn't seem like such a big mystery to me."

"That's because you don't know Ms. Huffington," she insisted. "My father says you can set your watch by her. She always comes to work exactly on time, an hour before anyone else. And she's always the last one to leave. She locks the doors, turns on the alarm system, and locks the gate on her way out. No one can get in after that except her or Father."

DETECTIVE ZACK

"Maybe people are breaking in at night," I suggested. "You know, through a window or door. Maybe they know how to get around the alarms somehow."

She raised one eyebrow. "It would be hard to believe that someone would break into Darkmoor Manor but not take anything."

I was just guessing. "Maybe they're breaking in just for fun."

When I said that, she laughed. "Wait until you see the museum." I didn't have to wait long. When the car rumbled past an iron gate in a stone wall, Stefanie squealed, "We're here!"

I stared past the raindrops rolling down my window as we rolled up to the curb. The big, square building looked like it was a hundred years old. The walls were made of giant stones. A giant-sized wooden door stood in the middle of the stones. It looked too heavy for six people to push open. There were windows along each side, a row of high ones and a row of low ones. But every window was crossed by big iron bars.

"It looks like a prison," I muttered.

"Very good, Zack," Mr. Townsend said. "That's exactly what it was."

Stefanie smiled sweetly at me. "Still think someone might be breaking in just for fun?" Then she laughed and reached past me to push the door open. "Come on! I want you to meet Ms. Huffington."

We wound our way through the people waiting to buy tickets and went straight to the door of an office. "I'm here, Ms. Huffington," Stefanie sang out.

A woman looked up from where she sat behind a desk. "I see that you are, Stefanie. And this would be your friend, Zackary?"

"It's just Zack, Ma'am," I responded. "Nice to meet you." The gray edges in her short brown hair made me think that Ms. Huffington was older than my mom but not as old as my grandma.

Stefanie whirled around the tiny room. "I didn't even know we were coming here today. But Dad surprised us. And it's a good thing—now Zack and I have two mysteries to solve."

"Ah yes," Ms. Huffington said, looking at me again. "The inspector from America." She talked kind of gruffly, but her eyes were smiling.

Just then, a man stuck his head in the room. "Ms. Huffington, George says there is a problem with a display. Can you spare a moment?"

"Certainly, Charles." Ms. Huffington stood and walked past us into the museum. She called over her shoulder to Stefanie. "Tell your father that I need to speak to him before you go."

"Right," Stefanie answered her. "Isn't she great?" she added to me.

"I guess," I said. "She seems really busy. And she doesn't seem like the type that would make up things—or believe in ghosts."

Stefanie stared after her friend. "She's not. She doesn't even like mysteries. She likes it when everything makes sense and there are no questions. George is the same way. He's the assistant manager."

I shook my head. "That makes it even stranger."

Stefanie led the way after them. "But Charles likes mysteries. He says that's why he's studying history in school—so he can solve mysteries about the past. He's only been here a few months." Suddenly, she grabbed my arm and pointed toward a group of people at the top of a stairway to a lower floor. "Come on. You have to hear this."

We rushed over and joined the group gathered around a college-aged girl. "Welcome to Darkmoor Manor," she was saying. "As we begin our tour, you need to know that Darkmoor was once a prison. These walls are made of stone three feet thick, and the bars on the windows are iron as thick as the trunk of a small tree. The most famous prisoner of Darkmoor was Edwin Murphey, the Duke of Marbury. He is also known as "The Disappearing Duke" or "Magic Murphey" because he did something everyone thought was impossible. He escaped from Darkmoor Prison."

She paused while several people gasped and others began whispering. Then she went on. "The stories say he made himself invisible and just walked past the guards. Or that he walked right through the walls by magic."

A man standing near her laughed. "Come on. It's simple. He slipped some money to one of the guards to open the door. That's not magic." Others laughed with him.

I reached into my pocket for my tape recorder and pushed the button. Stefanie saw what I was doing and laughed. "You don't need to do that," she whispered. "I know the whole tour-guide speech by heart."

The tour guide smiled and went on. "The only things Magic Murphey left behind were three clues carved into the stone wall of his cell. The legend says if you can figure out these clues, you can find Murphey's secret escape. But no one ever has. Maybe you will be the first to figure it out today as we tour Darkmoor Manor. Now, if you'll follow me down these stairs, we'll begin with a look at the old prison cells and some scenes from England's past."

As they walked away, Stefanie smiled. "See, Zack? I knew you would like this place."

She was right. I was beginning to like Darkmoor Manor a lot.

Note: In England, people drive on the left side of the road, from the right side of the car.

Clues About the Bible

How do we know that Bible stories tell us what really happened? Did a kid fight a giant-sized soldier with only a sling? Or did people make up that story as they retold the story of a regular sword fight?

Darkmoor Manor Mystery

Darkmoor Manor is built like a prison, because it was a prison once. Now it's a museum.

Ms. Huffington says that nearly every night things inside the museum are moved around. But no one can get inside.

The most famous prisoner of Darkmoor was Edwin Murphey, the Duke of Marbury. He is also known as "The Disappearing Duke" or "Magic Murphey" because he escaped from Darkmoor Prison. He left three clues carved on his stone wall.

Words to Remember

Turbulence: The bumpy air you find when a plane moves into an area where the air is moving in a different direction.

Boot: What people in England call the trunk of the car.

Mad: Sometimes it means really happy—at least it does in England.

CHAPTER THREE

Inspector Zack

I didn't want to leave Darkmoor Manor last night, but by the time Mr. Townsend took me to the hotel where Mom was, I was glad to see a bed. And it didn't take me long to get in it. "I'm just going to write a few things down," I told Mom. She picked up the phone to call Dad.

The next thing I knew, it was morning. We left early to go sightseeing, and I didn't get a chance to write anything down until we stopped in St. James Park. It's a beautiful green park next to Buckingham Palace. Buckingham Palace is a big, big house where the royal family lives. We didn't get to see the queen or anyone, but we did see the palace guards in those red uniforms and big black hats.

DETECTIVE ZACK

Mom wanted to look into some shops, so I sat down with my new notebook to write down everything that happened yesterday. Wait—I haven't even told you where I got the notebook—or even why Mr. Townsend took me to the hotel last night. Let me explain.

We hadn't been at Darkmoor Manor very long yesterday when Stef's mother was ready to go. "Come along, dear," she said to Mr. Townsend. "These people are ready to get to their hotel."

"I'm not," I said quickly.

Stefanie spoke quickly too. "Can we stay here while you take her to the hotel? We have a lot of things to talk about."

Mom shrugged. "It's OK with me, unless he's going to be a bother."

"No bother at all," Mr. Townsend said. "I'll bring him 'round later."

I remembered something else. "Mom, if you go by a store, I still need a new notebook."

Stefanie's dad raised one eyebrow. "What's this? A notebook? Planning a bit of writing, Zack?"

Stef answered first. "Father, I told you about Zack. He's the one who solves mysteries. He needs a notebook to write down the clues."

He nodded and smiled. "Ah yes. Our young inspector. Zack, I have just the thing for you. Walk this way, my boy."

I followed his long steps over to the gift shop, where he reached behind the counter and pulled out a small black notebook with the words "Darkmoor Manor" written across the front. "This ought to do the trick."

"Thank you," I said. "This is perfect."

He nodded slightly. "You'll need this as well, Inspector Zack." Then he handed me a black pencil—a black "Darkmoor Manor" pencil.

So that's what I'm writing in. I played back my tape recording from yesterday and remembered one more thing from the museum. Stef was showing me a letter signed by King Somebody the Second when Ms. Huffington came rushing over. "Let's not touch that," she said roughly. "One touch could destroy it."

Stefanie was hurt. "I know that! You're the one who taught me."

Ms. Huffington closed her eyes and took a breath. "My apologies, Stefanie. Of course you know to be careful." She rubbed the sides of her head. "I don't seem to be myself today. Are you teaching Zackary about the letters and other documents in our museum?"

Not Zackary—Zack, I said to myself. Out loud, I said, "How do you know if letters like this are real? How do you know that the king really signed this?"

"It's not always easy," Ms. Huffington admitted. "Some forgeries (for-jer-ies)—that's what we call it when a person creates a fake document to trick other people—are very difficult to detect."

Charles and George came over from where they were working and listened too. Ms. Huffington went on. "This is a real letter from the king. We compared the writing, the ink, and the paper to other letters from that time, and they are the same." She opened a file drawer and pulled out another old brown piece of paper. "This is a deed, or title, to the Carlawn Estate. It's a large plot of land with several farms and houses. It is operated or controlled by one person or family."

"You mean like a farm or a ranch in America?" I asked.

She nodded. "But here in England, many of these estates have been in certain important families for hundreds of years."

"What makes them important?" I asked.

George answered. "Usually, they are distant relatives of the royal family. Or someone to whom the king or queen has given a title such as earl or duke. And that title is passed on through the family. In this case, the owner of this estate would be known as the Earl of Carlawn."

Charles leaned past me and stared at the title. "Then this must be very valuable. If someone owned it, it would prove that the property is his and that he is rightfully the Earl of Carlawn."

"Yes, it would," Ms. Huffington agreed. "Except for one thing. This is a forgery—a fake."

Stefanie gasped. "How can you tell?" Charles crowded even closer.

Ms. Huffington pointed to the paper. "This paper is from the right time. And the handwriting is a very good copy of the original."

Charles almost looked mad. "Then how do you know it's a forgery?"

"The ink," she answered. "The ink used on this paper was not even invented yet when the original title to Carlawn was written." She put it back into the drawer. "We are planning an exhibit of titles soon. We want to show some real ones along with some forgeries."

Charles acted surprised. "The museum has some real titles? Where are the owners? Why don't they want them back?"

"Think about it, Charles," George said. "The families who owned those titles had all died. No one remains to claim the land or the title. When that happens, the land and the title return to the crown—that is, it becomes the property of the king or queen. Darkmoor is holding the actual papers because each one is a part of our history."

Last night, on the way back to the hotel, those old papers made me think about the Bible again and where it came from. Do you ever wonder where your Bible came from? I don't mean "from the store" or "a birthday present from Grandma." I mean, who wrote the words you read on those pages?

You always hear that the Bible is God's Word. Does that mean He wrote it? Did God write the story of David and Goliath? Or was it someone who saw the whole thing? Or did people just start repeating a story they heard someone else tell?

Did anyone check to see if any of those stories were forgeries—fake stories added just to make the Bible more interesting?

Maybe if they can tell that old letters or titles are fake, they can tell if the old stories of the Bible were really written at the right time. You know— that stories about David were written during the time David lived. And that stories about Moses were written in the time he lived. That would help prove that the stories we read in our Bible really did happen—not like the stories from Greece or Rome.

I wasn't even thinking about those questions this morning when Mom and I went to the London Museum. It's much bigger than Darkmoor, but Darkmoor has more mysteries. Anyway, we stopped in front of a display that held a big, thick book. The pages were open to show words written in a language I had never seen before.

Mom read the sign on the case. "It's a Gutenberg (Goo-ten-berg) Bible."

"Who's Bible?" I asked.

A man who works at the museum stepped over beside us. "Did you have questions? My name is Hopkins, and it would be a pleasure to assist you if I can."

Finally, I thought, *maybe I can find some answers. Someone who knows about a Bible this old should be able to tell me about where the Bible stories came from—and whether they are real or fake.*

I found some answers, all right. And it's even worse than I imagined.

CHAPTER FOUR

Something Terrible

I pointed to the big book in the display case and asked my question. "Mr. Hopkins, is that really a Bible?"

He smiled. "It is a Bible, but not just any Bible. Johann (Yo-hawn) Gutenberg invented the first printing press back in 1455. The first book he printed was a Bible. This is one of only a few that remain from Gutenberg's press."

I was impressed with that. "This is one of the first books ever printed? Wow, it's hard to imagine a world without books," I said to Mom. "Libraries wouldn't need many shelves."

"Oh, there were books before then," Mom said. "They were just written out by hand."

"That's right," Mr. Hopkins agreed. "Before that, all copies of books, even Bibles, were written out by hand."

"People really copied the whole Bible by hand?" I twisted my wrist and tried to imagine it. "My hand gets sore when I have to write out my spelling words five times each."

"They did," Mr. Hopkins said, "and it took a long time to finish even one book. Before the printing press, most people lived their whole lives without ever seeing or holding a Bible."

"Really?" I was surprised. "Then how did they know about the Bible stories? How did they know what to believe?"

Mom answered first. "Well, most churches had a copy of the Bible—or at least copies of parts of it."

"Oh, so people checked it out like a library book and took it home to read," I figured. "That's not too bad."

Mr. Hopkins shook his head. "No. Those hand-copied Bibles were very big and heavy. And very valuable. Usually they were chained to a big table in the church so no one could take them."

That made me frown. "So people had to stand right there in the church to read a Bible? It must have been hard to get many verses read."

"Harder than you think," he answered with a laugh. "Very few people in those days could read. And even for those who could, those Bibles were written in a different language than the one they spoke."

Mr. Hopkins went to answer another person's question, and Mom and I walked on to see the other exhibits. I kept thinking about what he said and by the time we got outside, I had another question.

"Mom, if people couldn't read or understand the words in their Bibles, then they didn't know anything. How did they learn about God in the first place?"

She had a smile with her answer. "Just like you did, Zack. You knew about God before you could read, didn't you?"

"Well, sure," I said. "You and Dad taught me about Jesus and Moses and Abraham and the stories in the Bible. And we learned by hearing the stories and singing songs in church."

"That's how most people learned about God in those days, Zack," she continued. "They listened when their pastors or priests told them the stories from the Bible and the words of promise from other verses. They heard how much God loved them, and they believed in Him. And they told other people. The stories in the Bible and God's plan to save humans were passed on from one person to another over and over. Through thousands of years they were repeated, until words were written and most people could read."

That made sense—almost. But if everyone learned about God by hearing the Bible stories, who told the first one? How do we know the stories written in our Bible are what really happened? How do we know they're not fakes? If it was thousands of years before any of the stories were even written down, there's no way to check them out.

Now you know why I'm worried about the Bible and its stories. This morning, it seemed like a bigger mystery than anything going on at Darkmoor Manor.

As I soon found out, I was wrong about that too.

Stefanie and her dad picked me up at the hotel on their way back to Darkmoor. As we pulled into a parking spot, Stef pointed to the front door of the museum. The front door was surrounded by people holding umbrellas. "What's with the crowd, Father? A new exhibit?"

"Humph," Mr. Townsend grunted. "No exhibit I know of."

As we got out, I pointed to the car next to us.

"Looks like that person has a cat too. And it must be a big one—look at the size of those paw prints!"

Then someone started toward us from the crowd, shouting as he came. It was Charles. "Mr. Townsend, Mr. Townsend! Something terrible has happened!"

Stef's dad stopped. "Well, out with it, Charles. What's happened? And where's Ms. Huffington?"

Charles took a deep breath. "That's just it, sir. Ms. Huffington didn't show up today. And she doesn't answer at home either. I think something dreadful has happened to her."

Stefanie gasped. "Oh no! She was right. She just knew something bad was going to . . ." She clamped her hand over her mouth to keep from saying anything else.

Mr. Townsend ignored her. "You mean Ms. Huffington has not been here at all? Then who opened the museum?"

"Well, er, no one, sir," Charles stammered as he looked back over his shoulder. "That's why the crowd is out here."

Mr. Townsend was already walking quickly to the museum door, shouting orders over his shoulder. "Charles, find George. Come, Stefanie. I may need you to be a tour guide."

Stefanie hurried after her dad. I hurried to

open the car door and get my backpack. At the same time, Charles was getting something from his car. "You must have a really big cat," I said, trying to be friendly.

He glanced at me like he had forgotten anyone was there. "Of course not," he said quickly. "I don't even like cats." Then he rushed off toward another car. I ran to catch up with Stefanie.

"We apologize for the delay in opening," Mr. Townsend was saying to the people waiting by the door. "Allow us to sort out a few problems; then we'll be ready to invite you inside."

As we went in, other employees got out of their cars and headed in too. Before long, the lights were on and people were rushing to get ready for the visitors. "George," Mr. Townsend called to the assistant manager, "check and make sure that everything is in shape downstairs. Charles, you check up here."

Stefanie rubbed her hands together. "Father, what about Ms. Huffington?"

"Just what I was wondering," he answered. We followed him over to the counter, where he picked up the phone and dialed a number.

"What do you think happened to Ms. Huffington?" I asked Stefanie while we waited. "You almost said something out by the car."

She looked around to be sure no one was listening. "Ms. Huffington was afraid something bad was going to happen to her. Or else that she was really going loony."

Before I could say anything, her dad put the phone down. "Well, Ms. Huffington is still not at home. Where could that woman have gone?"

"Dad," Stefanie asked, "are you going to call the police and tell them that Ms. Huffington is missing?"

"No, no, darling," he answered. "The police can't be bothered every time someone doesn't show up for work. I'm sure Ms. Huffington will be here soon, with a good story of why she was late." He turned away, muttering to himself. "At least, she'd better have a good story."

Just then, George appeared at the top of the stairs. "Mr. Townsend, I think you'd better come have a look at this."

Clues About the Bible

Who actually wrote the Bible? Who told the stories first?

If they can tell that old letters are fake, can they tell if the old stories of the Bible were really written at the time the story happened?

Before Bibles were printed, most people couldn't read or write, and most Bibles were locked in churches. People learned about God by listening to stories.

Darkmoor Manor Mystery

Ms. Huffington didn't show up for work. No one knows where she is.

Words to Remember

Forgeries: A fake document created to trick other people.

Estate: A large area of land operated or controlled by one person or family.

Titles: Important people were given an estate and a title like earl or duke, which was handed down through the family. Also, a title can be the piece of paper that shows that a person owns an estate.

CHAPTER FIVE

Inspector Brown's Bobbies

Stef and I followed her dad down the stairs to the large lighted case George was now standing beside. George didn't say a word as we arrived. He just stood there with a blank look on his face.

Stef's dad stopped and stared into the case. "Gone? They're all gone?"

George nodded. "It seems that they are. But look, sir. The case hasn't been damaged—and it's still locked."

"What's gone?" I asked Stefanie. "What was in there?"

"Old rare coins," she answered. "But how can they be gone if the case is still locked? Unless Ms. Huffington was right, and this place is haunted.

Who else could have taken those coins without even opening the case?"

Mr. Townsend looked at her but spoke to George. "George, who has the keys to the cases?"

"As far as I know, sir, only Ms. Huffington. And yourself, of course."

I saw the look on Mr. Townsend's face. Suddenly, I could think of a good answer to the clues in front of us—a much better answer than ghosts.

It looked like Mr. Townsend was thinking the same thing. He turned and headed back up the stairs. "George, the museum will not be opening today. Please inform the visitors outside. I believe I shall ring the police."

Stefanie turned to George. "Why is Father going to call the police? What are they going to do?"

He shrugged. "Look for clues, I suppose." Then he headed up the stairs too.

Stef and I followed him. "How can there be clues?" she asked. "Why bother calling the police?"

I stopped and grabbed her arm. "Stef, I don't think your dad believes that ghosts took those coins."

She looked confused. "I know. I don't either. But who could take coins out of that case without even unlocking it?"

"Ms. Huffington."

She was shocked. "Zack," she said with both hands on her hips, "I can't believe you said that. Ms. Huffington would never steal from Darkmoor."

"Stef, the clues all point to her. She's the only one who could get inside, the only one who could open that case, and she's gone. It looks like she took some valuable coins and ran away, hoping to sell the coins later for enough money to live without having to work."

She stared at me for a minute. I knew she wanted to be mad at me, but she knew I was right about the clues. Suddenly, she turned and ran up the stairs. "We'll just have to find clues that prove she didn't do it. Come on, Zack."

Her dad was hanging up the phone when we got there. Stef didn't waste any time. "Dad, do you really think Ms. Huffington took those things?"

He looked at me. "Do you think that's what the clues point to, Inspector Zack?"

I shrugged. "So far, they do."

He nodded and turned to Stefanie. "Darling, I know you and Ms. Huffington are friends. She's a friend of mine also. But it does seem odd that she would disappear the same day some very valuable items are missing. I know you don't want to think she did this. I don't want to either. When the police inspector arrives, let's let him make up his own mind about the clues."

Stefanie frowned and said, "Zack and I are going to collect clues to prove she didn't do it. Right, Zack?"

"Right," I agreed. *I just hope there are clues to find*, I added to myself.

When the police inspector—that's what they call a detective in England, by the way—and his men arrived, Mr. Townsend asked us to stay out of their way. So we did. We followed them around and stayed far enough away not to be a bother but close enough to hear.

"What is that bobby doing?" Stef asked me, pointing at one of the policemen.

I squinted at the guy. "How do you know his name is Bobby?"

"What?" She stared at me for a second, then laughed. "His name isn't Bobby. That's what we call police officers."

"Why?" I asked.

She shrugged. "I don't know. We just do."

I shook my head and watched the officer behind the ticket counter for a moment. He held a magnifying glass close to his eye and stared at the drawers and counter top. "I think he's looking for scratches or scraps that would show that someone tried to force those drawers open to steal things from there."

"Why?" Stef asked. "We told them that the only things stolen were from that one coin case."

"He's not looking to see if something was taken. He's looking to see if someone tried to break the drawers open to take other things. You should hope he finds something," I reminded her. "If a stranger broke in here, he wouldn't know where the valuable things were. He'd look in every drawer."

She got the point. "But someone who works here would know exactly where to get what they wanted. Someone like Ms. Huffington."

We sat down on the stairs to watch Inspector Brown inspect the coin case. As he stared at it closely, he asked, "Do you have fingerprints on file for each of your employees?"

Mr. Townsend nodded. "I require that for all employees. Everything in the museum is valuable."

Inspector Brown nodded to one of his officers who brought a brush and began painting it with powder. "Fingerprint powder," I whispered to Stef.

"Let's hope they don't find one of Ms.

Huffington's," she whispered back.

"They probably will," I said. Stef's face told me she was getting angry. "Hey, she works here. Her fingerprints must be all over the place. That won't prove anything."

Inspector Brown was listening to Stef's dad talk about Ms. Huffington. "She's been the manager here for ten years. I have trusted her like I would my own wife. She's never tardy for work, never leaves early. First to arrive, last to leave—that was Ms. Huffington."

Inspector Brown was taking notes—in his notebook, I noticed. "And today she hasn't shown up at all. Did she mention any new problems recently? Unhappy visitors here, problems at home, anything?"

Mr. Townsend thought for a moment, then shook his head. "No, nothing unusual."

Stef nearly exploded. "Father! What about those strange things that were happening at night? It was really starting to drive her bonkers!"

The inspector looked at Stefanie. "Bonkers?"

Stef looked at her dad. He nodded. "Ms. Huffington has been telling us for weeks that something strange is going on here at night. She claimed that on many mornings, when she arrives to work, things are moved from the night before—drawers open, objects moved, things knocked over. She even has suggested the museum might be haunted. I thought that perhaps she was growing forgetful."

Inspector Brown thought about that. "It is rather hard to imagine someone breaking in here just for a joke or two. But I'm not a believer in ghosts either." He pointed to two officers standing nearby. "Let's do a complete search of the building, inside and out. We're looking for signs of a break in. Begin down here." He stood to walk back upstairs as the two bobbies (It still sounds strange to me!) turned to walk down the hall. "Now, Mr. Townsend, let us see if the chaps have learned anything of interest from your other workers."

Stefanie and I watched the two bobbies walk down the hallway. "I guess if these bobbies find clues that someone has been coming in, then Ms. Huffington wouldn't be suspected," she finally said.

I agreed. "And if someone has broken in, they won't be hard to find."

Stef tilted her head. "Why do you think that?"

I looked around at the stone walls again. "All we'll have to do is follow the bulldozer tracks. Because that's what it would take to break into this place. Come on, let's see what Inspector Brown's bobbies found upstairs."

CHAPTER SIX

Magic Murphey's Cell

We got up to the museum office in time to hear Charles answer a question. "I've only been here for a few months. I've been studying history in college, and Mr. Townsend hired me as an assistant to the assistant manager."

Stef's dad spoke up. "Charles has been a real help to us. He knows the history of some of the things in this museum better than I do. And the history of Darkmoor prison."

Charles nodded slightly. "Darkmoor has always been a hobby of mine."

Mr. Townsend smiled. "Well, it's a good thing for us. Especially now that Ms. Huffington is—uh—out of touch."

DETECTIVE ZACK

Inspector Brown had another question. "Charles, are you friends with Ms. Huffington outside of work? Have you been to her home?"

"Oh no," Charles answered. "She's a wonderful person to work for, but I've never been to her house. I spend most of my time at school."

Stefanie got bored quickly. "Come on. I'll show you the rest of the museum."

"Wait," I said. "Let's see if we can find out what clues the police found. Do you think your dad will let us stay and listen?"

Stefanie shook her head. "Any second now, he'll say something like, 'Why don't you two run along while the inspector and I have a little chat.' "

Just then, a police officer stepped in and motioned Inspector Brown over. He spoke quietly, but I listened. "No signs of breaking in either inside or out around the building. We did find one shoeprint in the mud near a back window, but there was no evidence of tampering with the window itself."

Inspector Brown nodded, then walked over to stand beside Mr. Townsend. Stef's dad cleared his throat and said, "Why don't you two run along while the inspector and I have a little chat."

Stef turned to me. "Told you," she said as she led the way out the door.

"That's OK," I decided. "You still haven't given me a real tour of this place. Maybe we can find some clues those bobbies missed."

We headed back down the stairs, and Stefanie began her tour-guide speech. "Each of these little rooms—what used to be prison cells—is filled with things from different times in England's history." She pointed to the first room on the right. "Those are from the time of King Arthur and the Knights of the Round Table."

I could see that. That room still had its prison bars, which kept the visitors away from the swords and shields and suits of armor—and a horse with a knight on top. "Is the horse made of metal like the armor?" I asked as I tried to open the cell door.

"No," she answered. "It's stuffed. And don't bother trying to open those doors. They're locked up with a big key that Ms. Huffington keeps in the safe."

The next room had things like bows and arrows, wagon carts, and old dresses. Everything was shown in glass cases or carefully out of reach beyond the cell bars. "This stuff looks like it came from the days of Robin Hood," I said, before she could begin her tour-guide speech.

"Good guess, Inspector," she teased. Then she led the way to a room that was nearly empty. But the cell door was open. "This is a new exhibit in the museum. This room shows how a prisoner lived when Darkmoor was a prison. In fact, this was Magic Murphey's cell."

"This I have to see," I said as I walked inside. There was nothing in the cell but a small wobbly wooden table, a stool to go with it, and a thin straw mattress for a bed. "No wonder Magic Murphey had to escape. He was probably bored out of his mind."

Then I heard a screeching sound behind me, followed by a crash. I jumped and spun around just in time to see Stefanie pull a big key out of the cell door. The cell door that was now closed. "Now you have to escape, too," she said with a laugh.

I walked over and grabbed the bars of the door. "Did he really escape from inside this cell?" I tried to shake the door, but all that shook was my bones.

"No," she admitted, "not from in there. They say that his door was unlocked. He escaped from somewhere out here. But he did carve his three clues on the wall in there. Right over by the table."

Of course, I had to see them. And I guess Stefanie did, too, because she unlocked the door and slid it back by the cell bars where it usually was. "It's all part of the tour," she said. "When the visitors go in to look at the clues, you pull this bar and the door slides shut with a bang. They usually think it's fun, especially since Magic Murphey's clues are so boring. I mean, what is that supposed to be a picture of anyway?"

I stared at the first scratching on the wall. "This one looks like an arrow pointing up. And the second one has an arrow pointing down. In the third clue, the arrow is curving to the right."

"Sure," she agreed, "that part's easy. What is that other drawing by the arrows?"

I frowned. "It looks kind of like a flat circle. You know, like you'd see if you held up a plate or a ring. It's like a . . . basketball hoop when you're looking at it from the free-throw line."

"Basketball hoop?" Stefanie looked at me as if I was from another planet.

I stared back at her. "You have heard of basketball, haven't you? You know—you dribble down the court and shoot the ball at the basket?"

She looked as if she was going to be sick. "You play this game by drooling?"

That even sounded sick to me. "No, no. Not drooling—dribbling. It's different. I'll show you."

She backed away. "No, thank you. Maybe later. Much later."

Have you ever tried to explain basketball without either a ball or a hoop? I gave up before I even started and followed her out of the cell. "Maybe we should stick with games we both know. Is anyone playing soccer this time of year?"

She walked over and sat on a bench under a window. "Soccer?" she asked. "Oh yes. Football. People are always playing football in England."

I jumped up on the bench beside her and hit my head on something. "Ouch! What is that?"

Stefanie looked up. "It's a torch. You know, the kind they used for light before electricity."

"Oh, right." The torch was attached to the wall right beside the window. It looked a little like the Olympic torch you see during the Olympic Games. Except this one wasn't all shiny gold. It was made of some kind of dark metal. I reached over up to touch it, and the torch moved. "Hey, did I break it?"

"No, the torch is sitting in a stand that holds it away from the hall. If they needed to, they could take the torch part out and carry it around." Stefanie started her tour-guide speech again. "The torch is filled with twigs and straw that have been soaked in oil or wax so they would burn longer. By the way, Father and Mother are going to a big football match the day after tomorrow. Do you want to go?"

Did I ever! "Sure! That would be great! I'll ask my mom." Then I remembered something. "Wait a minute—Mom is planning for us to go on an overnight tour of castles the same day."

Now Stefanie got excited. "Really? I love castles. I wish I could go with you."

That gave me an idea. "Why don't you ask your parents if you can go with my mom, and I'll ask my mom if I can stay with your parents!" We both laughed, but it was almost a good idea. "Why don't we both ask if we can go with the other. Then we'll decide which to go on." Stef agreed.

Outside, it was starting to rain again. But I still had to try something. I stuck my head between the bars and out into the rain. "Hey, look. My head is escaping!"

Stefanie rolled her eyes. "Zack, I'm getting wet. Close the window, please."

I pulled my head back in. "Close the window? What am I supposed to do—stack rocks in front of it?" Then I saw the glass. "Oh, there's a glass window too."

"Of course," Stefanie said. "You didn't think we just let the rain and cold in, did you?"

I pulled the glass window closed. "Hey, it doesn't even lock. How does that keep anyone out?"

DETECTIVE ZACK

"It doesn't, silly," Stefanie explained. "What lock would keep someone out if they could bend or break those iron bars?"

"Good point," I admitted. Then I jumped off the bench and landed in front of her. But before I could say another word, the whole room exploded with noise.

Darkmoor Manor Mystery

Valuable coins are missing from a display case that is still locked. Only Ms. Huffington and Mr. Townsend have keys to the case.

Ms. Huffington is still missing.

The police found no signs of a break-in, either inside or out around the building. That's not good news for Ms. Huffington.

Magic Murphey's clues: Flat circles with arrows. What kind of clues are those?

Words to Remember

Bobbies: What people in England call police officers.

Football: The game we call soccer in America.

CHAPTER SEVEN

Scrambled Messages

My head was still ringing when the Townsends dropped me off at the hotel tonight. I'll explain about that in a minute. Right now, I don't know which is more confusing—the Darkmoor Manor mystery or the mystery about the Bible. I told Mom about the police and everything. She shook her head. "This must really be upsetting Stefanie. I hope her friend is OK. Why don't you invite Stefanie to go with us on the castle tour this weekend?"

"I will," I agreed. "But she's already invited me to stay with her family and go to a big soccer game."

"You would enjoy that." She patted my arm

and went to comb out her wet hair. "You two decide and let me know."

"Mom," I asked a few minutes later, "remember what we talked about this morning? About how people just remembered and repeated the stories from the Bible for hundreds of years before anyone wrote them down?"

She nodded.

"Well, it made me think about a game Mrs. Lin made us play in school last week. We were all lined up against the chalkboard, with me on one end of the line and Luke at the other end. That wasn't how we started, but after Luke's hair turned white when I accidentally dropped the chalkboard eraser—well, you know how teachers are."

Mom shook her comb at me. "I know how the two of you are. Really, Zack."

I decided to hurry on with my story. "Anyway, Mrs. Lin turned to me first. 'Zack,' she said, 'think of a short message, then whisper it to Sara. Then Sara, repeat the message Zack tells you to the next person. Each of you will repeat the same message—in a whisper—to the next person. When the message gets to the end, Luke will repeat the message out loud. Then Zack will tell us if that was the message he sent. Go ahead, Zack.'"

"Well, I couldn't think of any message to send. But when ·Mrs. Lin started tapping her shoe, I whispered the first thing on my mind to Sara. She passed it on, and so did the next person and the next person. Finally, it got to Luke. He listened, then shook his head and repeated it out loud. 'I have soap and pearls on my dress.' "

Mom almost laughed out loud. "What!"

I held up my hands. "But that wasn't my message. I told Sara, 'I hope we get out early for recess.' Luke heard, 'I have soap and pearls on my dress.' It was kind of funny then. But now it makes me think. If one message being repeated across a room can get so messed up so quick, what might have happened to all the Bible's messages and stories when they were repeated for hundreds of years? Are the stories we read anything like what really happened?"

Mom looked at me in the mirror while she combed. "Zack, what would you do tonight if you were bored? How would you entertain yourself?"

I wasn't sure what this had to do with my question, but I answered. "I'd probably read a book or watch TV."

"What did you do in the evening when you were at Thunder Mountain Camp?"

I thought for a second. "We went to campfire

and sang songs and watched skits or listened to stories."

She kept asking and combing. "And what about when we were camping in Utah or at Dinosaur Camp? What did you and Kayla do in the evening after we ate supper?"

That was another strange question. "We explored some with our flashlights. Then we came and sat by the fire and talked or listened to Dad tell stories."

Finally, she put the comb down and turned around. "Remember that the people who lived in the hundreds of years you're talking about lived a lot like the way we camped. In the evenings or on celebration days, they didn't go rent a video or play the latest computer game. Their fun was listening to people tell stories."

I hadn't thought of that. "You're right, Mom. Stories were important to them. What . . ."

"Let me finish," she said. "So when people told stories, they didn't skip to the good parts or leave out sections to make it shorter. They told the whole story, exactly the way they had heard it. They told it waving their arms and jumping up and down. They told it with different voices for different people and with swords or sticks or whatever they needed. Telling stories was very important. It was how they learned, it was how they had fun, it was how they remembered their family history, and it was how they remembered God."

I got it. "So it wasn't like me remembering something that happened in school or being able to say a memory verse. They heard these stories over and over, all their lives."

Mom smiled. "That's right. And the job of remembering was very important. The most important person in any family was the leader. He was called the patriarch (pay-tree-ark). Abraham was the patriarch of his family, and he remembered all the stories. And Abraham's family was more than just his wife and children. It was all his relatives, like Lot and all his servants and the people who worked for him. They were hundreds of people who camped with Abraham everywhere he went."

I remembered the story. "That's right. Abraham had a big family before he even had any kids. Then Isaac was in charge of the family after Abraham died, right?"

"Right," she agreed. "Isaac was the next patriarch. He knew all the family stories. And remember what happened when he got old?"

I thought for a second. "Jacob and Esau started

fighting about who would get the birthright blessing. I never did understand what that was all about."

"Well, now you do!" Mom declared. "The birthright blessing went to the person who would take over the family next. The person who would be in charge of all the people and animals. It was his job to make sure everyone learned to follow God."

Now it made sense. "The birthright blessing gave him the right to tell the stories. Thanks, Mom. I've got to write this down." So that's what I did.

Now, about the explosion of noise in the basement at Darkmoor Manor: the shrieking sound was so loud, I thought my ears were going to cave in. I tried to pull my head down into my jacket, but that didn't help. The sound seemed to be coming from everywhere. "What is it?" I shouted to Stefanie. I'm sure she didn't hear me. I could barely hear myself, and she had both hands over her ears.

But she answered by pointing to the ceiling. I looked up and saw a small, round white box that looked like the smoke detector in my room at home. "Do you think it's a fire?" I shouted.

She just waved for me to follow and ran back toward the stairs. I was right behind her. Just as we got to the top of the stairs, the alarms stopped. We ran into the office just in time to hear Inspector Brown say, "The alarm system seems to be working properly."

One of his bobbies holding the phone nodded. "The alarm was received at the station."

Stef walked over to her father. "What's going on? There's not a fire, is there?"

He gave her a quick smile. "Oh no. Actually, you and Zack set the alarms off."

"We didn't touch any displays or anything," she protested.

He pointed to the smoke detector on the ceiling of the office. "You know how those work—they sense smoke from a fire. Well, the ones in the museum here are also motion detectors. They detect movement as well as smoke. If they sense that something or someone is moving, then the alarm goes off here and at the police station. Even when you unlock the front door, you have only forty-five seconds to punch in the right code on the alarm box here in the office or the alarms go off."

"And we set it off by moving downstairs." Stefanie flopped down onto a chair. "That's why you never believed Ms. Huffington," she said quietly. "If things were moved during the night, the motion detectors would have gone off. And that's why Ms. Huffington was so confused about it. She knew the alarms should have gone off, but they never did."

Stefanie's dad nodded. "So that's it, then," he said to Inspector Brown. "You tell me that there are no signs of a break-in, no signs that any other display cases were opened, and that the alarm systems were working. So whoever stole the coins came in through a locked door, turned off the alarm system, opened a locked case, locked it again, turned the alarm system back on, and locked the door on their way out."

The inspector nodded. "That's what the facts say so far. We'll stay on it and see what turns up." He reached for the phone and dialed the police station. "Send a car 'round to . . ." he read an address off a piece of paper.

"That's Ms. Huffington's house," Stef wailed to her dad. "They can't just go and arrest her! I know she didn't do anything wrong!"

Clues About the Bible

 If a simple message can get messed up by being repeated, how can stories not change when they've been told hundreds of times?

 Telling and remembering stories was different in Bible times. It was how people learned and were entertained. The leader of the family was supposed to make sure the family stories were remembered and passed on.

Darkmoor Manor Mystery

 There are no signs of a break-in, and no signs that any other display cases were opened. The alarm systems work.

 Whoever stole the coins came in through a locked door, turned off the alarm system, opened a locked case, locked it again, turned the alarm system back on, and locked the door on their way out.

 The alarms should have gone off when things moved at night. That's why Ms. Huffington was so confused.

Words to Remember

 Patriarch: The leader and most important person in a family in Bible times.

 Motion detectors: Smoke detectors sense smoke. Motion detectors sense movement.

CHAPTER EIGHT

Setting a Trap

Mr. Townsend stepped over to Stef and pulled a handkerchief from his pocket. "Darling," he said, as he wiped the tears off her face, "they're not going to arrest her. They just want to find her—like you do."

Inspector Brown was off the phone by then, and he agreed. "We'll know a lot more about what's gone on here when we can speak to her. We need to know what happened that she couldn't come to work today—or even call in to report."

Stef looked at the inspector. "Do you really think Ms. Huffington stole those coins?" she asked with a sniff.

Inspector Brown frowned. "A number of things

could have happened. She may know nothing about it. She may have been forced to open the museum and case for some other person."

I spoke up. "She could have been forced to steal those things by someone who promised to hurt one of her family or friends if she didn't."

The inspector looked at me, then at Mr. Townsend, who was frowning and thinking. "She does have an aunt who lives in Westchester," Mr. Townsend finally said. "Someone should call."

Inspector Brown was already writing it down.

Stefanie seemed to feel better. "Inspector, what if Ms. Huffington isn't home? What will you do?"

"Since we have reason to believe that something is wrong, and since we need her story for this investigation, we'll have to force our way in and inspect the house to see if anything seems odd."

Stefanie nodded. "Well, if you do, be careful not to step on Rangoon."

Now Inspector Brown was confused. "Be careful not to step on whom?"

"Rangoon," Stefanie answered. "Ms. Huffington's big yellow cat. He usually sleeps in front of the stove." Then she got a sad look on her face. "Of course, he might not be there. If she really ran off, Rangoon would be with her. She would never leave without him."

Inspector Brown looked at her. "You've been to her home quite often, haven't you?"

Stefanie nodded.

"How about if you kids come with us and look for this Rangoon?" he asked. Stefanie nodded, and they both turned to her dad.

He seemed too surprised to think. "Well, uh, it seems, perhaps . . . are you sure they won't be a bother?" he finally asked.

"Not at all," Inspector Brown said, putting his notebook away. "Stefanie can tell us whether or not things about the house seem normal."

"Very well," Mr. Townsend finally agreed. "I'll see you both back here shortly."

Since I knew I might never ride in a British police car again, I pulled out my tape recorder as soon as I got buckled into my seat. Inspector Brown saw it. "Creating your own souvenir, I see. Good thinking."

I pushed the button to record, and by the time we arrived at Ms. Huffington's house, I had recorded the Inspector Brown talking about a robbery at a hat shop, a traffic jam on the Tower Bridge, and his cat named Monty.

"You two wait here in the car until I give you a signal," he said as we pulled up behind another police car next to a small cottage. "I don't think there will be any problems, but I want to be safe."

I rolled down my window when he stepped out. A bobby was waiting. "There's no answer at the door," he reported. "Shall we have a go at getting inside?"

Inspector Brown spoke on the other car's radio for a moment, then signaled to the bobby waiting by the door. In just a few seconds, the door opened and the officer disappeared inside. A minute later, he was back, shaking his head at the inspector.

"Come along, now," Inspector Brown called to us. "There seems to be no one home." But before we could open the doors, a big yellow furrball landed right on the hood of the car.

"Rangoon!" Stefanie cried.

"Merr-ow?" the big cat answered. It walked right up to the windshield to stare at her, leaving big muddy paw prints all along the way.

"It's Rangoon," Stefanie called to Inspector Brown. "Now you can be sure that Ms. Huffington didn't take the coins and run—she'd never leave Rangoon behind. Come here, baby," Stefanie said to the cat. He was already in her arms, purring like a chain saw.

Inspector Brown sighed. "Cats with muddy feet just seem to love my bonnet," he said as he patted the car hood.

This time, I figured it out before I asked. They call the truck of a car the boot and the hood of a car the bonnet.

A walk through the house found Rangoon something to eat, but it didn't tell us much else. "It looks just like Ms. Huffington always keeps it," Stefanie announced, "perfectly clean, with everything put away properly."

We decided to take the cat with us. But Stefanie's dad didn't think it was a good idea for her to take the cat home. "Rangoon might scare away your own cat," he explained. "Why don't we fix him a place to stay here at Darkmoor? There's a lot of room for him to explore outside, and he can sleep in the old horse stable."

Stefanie and I took the cat around to the back of the museum and made him a bed of hay in the old stable. "He's feeling right at home," I said, when Rangoon started purring loud enough to rattle the walls.

Stef kept petting him. "I just know that Ms. Huffington wouldn't have left him. Someone must have kidnapped her."

"But why?" I asked. "What does she have besides the museum? And why wouldn't they steal more than just a few coins if all they wanted was money? They had to know that your father would have the locks changed so they couldn't come back."

Stefanie stared off into the distance. "Unless it's the same people who were coming in at night before. Zack, something really was going on. I don't know how, but something weird was happening."

I stood up. "Then what we need is a trap. And I just got a great idea for one."

Stefanie stood up beside me. "This time, I don't care how weird your trap is—I'm ready to try anything."

I guess she still remembered the traps I set that didn't work. Well, this one was sure to work—if someone really was breaking into the museum at night.

By the time the last visitors were leaving, Stef and I were ready. We raced downstairs with some string and my tape recorder. "Tell me again how this is going to work," she said.

"First, we have to set the cell door to close by itself," I reminded her.

She pulled the handle-shaped lever, and the door scraped shut. "That part is easy," she said as she pushed it back.

I pulled out some of the string. "Now all we

have to do is tie this string across the doorway into the cell so that when someone goes in, their foot pulls the string and the string pulls the lever."

A few minutes later, we were ready to try it out. "Here I go," Stef said as she walked into the cell. The string caught on her right shoe and pulled. Before she tripped, it came loose. But not before it had pulled the handle. The door closed right behind her.

"Great! It works," I said.

"Except for one thing," Stefanie insisted. "Why would whoever comes in the museum want to come in this cell?"

I pulled out my tape recorder. "That's why we set this on the counter upstairs and let it record all afternoon. I set it on slow speed, so this tape of people talking will last six hours. When we leave, this recorder will be in here playing that tape for six hours. If someone comes into the museum before six hours go by, they'll hear the recorded voices and come to investigate. Once they step through that door and pull that string, they'll be locked up tight until morning."

I pressed the play button. "Then the person who took the coins and Ms. Huffington will be trapped."

CHAPTER NINE

Good Trap, Wrong Person

After Darkmoor Manor closed, Stefanie took Mom and me to the Tower of London on the Underground. That's what they call their subway. You know what a subway is—those little trains that run mostly underground in a lot of big cities.

"I'm glad you're with us," Mom told Stefanie when we got off at the Tower Hill Station. "I would have gotten us lost before we even got off the Underground."

The Tower was really interesting. It's really a whole set of buildings with a wall around them all. They're some of the oldest buildings in London. The White Tower used to be the royal palace and a prison—at the same time.

DETECTIVE ZACK

On the way back, I told Stefanie how Mom explained about how people told and remembered the stories in the Bible. Stef wasn't convinced. "But what about those old stories from Greece and Rome? Remember—every time the stories were told, the people in them got stronger and braver. By the time they were written down, not much that really happened was left. How do we know the same thing didn't happen with the Bible stories?"

Mom thought for a second. "Maybe that did begin to happen once. Remember how Joseph's brothers and his father and their families moved to Egypt because of the famine?"

I remembered. "But another pharaoh made them all slaves."

"Right. The Israelites were in Egypt for hundreds of years. They must have been forgetting the stories about Adam and Eve, about Noah, and even about Abraham. So when God chose Moses to lead them back to their own land, He also chose Moses to write down all their stories."

Stefanie snapped her fingers. "Of course! Moses grew up in Pharaoh's palace. He learned how to read and write. Probably not very many people knew how."

Mom smiled. "That's right. The first five books

of the Bible are known as the 'Books of Moses.' Of course, Moses didn't see Creation or the Flood. But, either God helped him remember those stories the right way or else God told him the stories again."

That made me smile. I could just imagine God and Moses sitting around a campfire in the desert. God would be telling stories, and Moses would be writing as fast as he could in his notebook.

Last night when Mr. Townsend picked Stefanie up, he promised that we could go with him to Darkmoor early in the morning. "We want to check on Rangoon—and some other stuff," Stefanie explained.

"I don't mind, if you want to get up that early. Zack, are you in on this plan to beat the rooster in the morning?"

"Yes, sir!" I answered. "I'll be ready when you stop to pick me up."

I don't know about the roosters, but the rest of the birds were already up by the time we got to Darkmoor Manor the next morning. Hundreds of them were in the trees around us, singing like the first-grade choir—each one was carrying its own tune. "What are they so cheerful about?" I grumbled, still trying to keep my eyes open.

We followed Mr. Townsend into the dark museum and waited by the door until he switched on the lights. "Just a minute," he said from the office door. "Who switched off the alarm system?"

That made my eyes pop open. But what we heard next almost made them pop out. "Ello," someone called from downstairs.

Mr. Townsend froze. Stef jumped up and down. "It worked! We caught him!"

Her dad grabbed her arm. "What worked? Who is that? What is going on here!"

Stef explained. "We set a trap to catch the person who's been coming in at night. It has to be the same person who stole those coins—and Ms. Huffington."

For a second, he stared at her—then at me. "You . . . well, come on!" We hurried down the stairs to the last cell on the end. There, leaning against the bars, was the thief.

"George!" Stefanie was shocked. But not for long. "Where is Ms. Huffington? What have you done with her?"

George looked very tired. He opened his mouth, but before any sounds came out, Mr. Townsend spoke. "Really, George. I expected more from you."

"Perhaps I could explain," George said patiently. "I also do not believe that Ms. Huffington had anything to do with the stolen coins. And I do

think something has been going on here at night.
So, using the keys you gave me yesterday," he said
to Mr. Townsend, "I stopped by last night just to
check things out. I came in through the front door,
turned off the alarm, and began to look around.
Then I heard voices down here."

"Voices?" Mr. Townsend was shocked again.
"Do you mean there were other people here as
well?"

"Not exactly," I answered.

"It was part of the trap," Stefanie explained.
"We left Zack's tape recorder playing in the cell."

Mr. Townsend looked at George. He nodded,
picked up my tape recorder, and reached through
the bars to hand it to me. "I believe the batteries
may be dead."

Stefanie went on. "Then we rigged the door
here with this string so that if someone came in to
see about the voices, he would trip on the string
and the door would slide shut."

"It worked quite well," George added. "It just
caught the wrong person. You can ring the missus
and ask. I'm quite sure she'll be happy to know
that I've been locked in a prison cell all night and
not been off running about the town."

Mr. Townsend's shoulders sagged. "Stefanie, I
know you two were trying to help, but this is . . ."

"Excuse me, sir," George interrupted, "but we didn't plan this exhibit with sleepovers in mind. If you could unlock the door, I'll be off to the W.C."

Now, even I felt bad for George. W.C. is one English name I already know. That's what they call a bathroom. Stef says that "W.C." stands for "water closet." She didn't know why they would call it a water closet. It's more fun to flush in their bathrooms though. Instead of pushing a handle on the tank, you pull on a chain that hangs from the ceiling. Don't you wish you had one in your bathroom?

Anyway, Mr. Townsend made us promise not to set any more traps without telling him. "My traps don't always work," I admitted.

He shook his head. "Nonsense, my boy. This one worked fine. Keep at it—just let me know what's going on."

George called his wife to explain and stayed until Charles arrived before he went home to change clothes. "I still think he might have done it," Stef said as we walked back toward the museum office. "He could have been coming in all along, just to fool Ms. Huffington."

I didn't think so. "Remember, he couldn't even get in until your father gave him the keys to the door yesterday."

Just then, the phone rang. "It's for Mr. Townsend," Charles announced. "Has anyone seen Mr. Townsend?"

"He's in the office," Stefanie answered. By the time we got there, her dad was hanging up the phone. He didn't look happy.

"That was Inspector Brown. It seems that they've found Ms. Huffington's car."

Stefanie's eyes lighted up. "And her? Did they find her?"

He shook his head. "No, I'm afraid not. They found her car at the airport, but there's no trace of her or the coins." He was still shaking his head as he walked out. "It's a real shame."

Stefanie didn't understand. "Why is that bad news?" she asked.

I tried to explain. "Since her car is at the airport, it looks even more like she stole the coins, drove to the airport, and flew off to some other country. Just leaving her car like that makes it seem like she had no plans to come back. Ever."

Clues About the Bible

When the Hebrews had been in slavery in Egypt for hundreds of years, God asked Moses to write down all their old stories so they wouldn't be forgotten or remembered wrong. After all, Moses grew up in Pharaoh's palace. He knew how to read and write.

Moses didn't see Creation or the Flood, but either God helped him remember those stories the right way or else God told him the stories again.

Darkmoor Manor Mystery

Ms. Huffington could have been forced to open the museum door and that case by some other person.

Rangoon was home, so maybe Ms. Huffington didn't run off.

If someone really was coming into the museum at night, a great trap might catch them.

Sometimes, a great trap doesn't work like you thought it would.

Ms. Huffington's car at the airport makes it seem even more likely she took the rare coins and ran.

Words to Remember

Bonnet: The part of a car you open to see the engine. In America, we call it the hood.

W.C.: Water closet. That's what they call a bathroom in England.

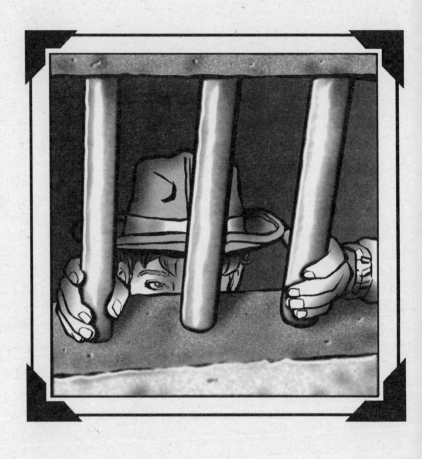

CHAPTER TEN

The Thousand-Year Test

"But she would never leave Rangoon," Stefanie wailed. "I just know it."

What else could I say? "We'll keep trying," I told her.

A few minutes later, we found something else to think about—Rangoon! The goofy cat kept coming in and running around in the museum. Stefanie's dad saw him first.

"Stefanie, what is that cat doing sitting on the king's throne? Get him out of here, please."

We chased Rangoon down and took him out three times. He seemed to think it was great fun. Every time, he'd find his way back inside—with a group of visitors or between the bars of an open window.

"There he is again," I called to Stefanie from the top of the stairs. "I think he went into the office."

"Oh no. Father will kill him this time—or us." We raced to the door and burst in. "We'll get him," Stef said without looking up. I just froze. The person sitting at the desk was not her father.

It was a gray-haired woman with a friendly smile. "Tell me whom you're looking for, and I'll help," she said.

"Oops." Stefanie's face turned red. "Pardon us. I thought you were my father." That sounded strange, so she tried to explain. "I don't mean I thought *you* were my father. I thought the cat was in here." Her face turned redder. "I don't mean I thought *the cat* was my father . . ." Finally, she stopped and covered her face with her hands.

The woman grinned. I smiled back. "What she's trying to ask is, have you seen a big yellow cat in here?"

"No, I haven't. But I've been staring at these papers for so long an elephant could have come in and hidden itself without me noticing. Is this cat a pet of yours? Shall we get down and look under the furniture?"

She started to bend down from her chair, but Stefanie came back to life. "No, no, don't do that.

We're just watching the cat for a friend. He'll show up somewhere. This is my father's museum. I'm Stefanie, and this is my friend Zack."

The woman nodded politely. "I'm Mrs. Tipton. Your father asked me to stop by and look at these handwritten copies of a Shakespeare (shakespear) play to see if I can tell when they were written."

"What kind of play?" I asked.

"A play written by William Shakespeare," she answered. "He was one of England's greatest writers. He wrote many plays that are performed in theaters all over the world. These papers don't seem to be handwritten by Shakespeare himself but could be copies made by people who worked with him. If they are, they would be quite valuable."

I walked over and looked at the papers. "How can you tell whether or not they are?"

"By the mistakes, mostly," she answered. "When a person copies things by hand, like this play, they usually copy it without paying close attention. They copy mistakes made by the last copier without even noticing."

That made me think about the Bible stories being written down and copied. Did they make mistakes too?

Mrs. Tipton looked closely at the page in front of her. "I'm beginning to think this copy was made many years after Shakespeare. It seems to have all the mistakes we usually see in early copies, plus some new ones."

This was starting to worry me. "Do people who copy by hand always make mistakes?" I asked her.

"Not always," Mrs. Tipton answered. "But copy something enough times, and mistakes creep in."

I slumped down onto a chair. Stefanie knew what I was thinking. "We've been trying to solve a mystery about the Bible," she explained. "We've been to Israel and seen the places where the Bible stories happened. But we don't know if what's in our Bible's today is the same as what really happened or what God really wanted someone to write."

Mrs. Tipton leaned back in the chair and nodded. "I see. Since those stories were copied over and over, you think that mistakes may have changed what God wanted to say."

"Right," I said. "After all, there aren't any original books to compare them to. First, the stories were just told and remembered; then they were written down. But that was thousands of years ago. They must have been copied hundreds and hundreds of times. Who knows how many mistakes are there now. For all I know, Goliath was no bigger than I am, and David fought him with a soccer ball."

"You mean a football," Stefanie said.

Mrs. Tipton thought for a minute. "Zack, studying old English manuscripts is part of my job. But I have studied the manuscripts of the Bible. What do you think happened after the fight between David and Goliath?"

I thought for a second. "Everyone started talking about it. I remember, because it made King Saul mad. He thought everyone liked David better than him."

She nodded. "That's right. Remember, in those days, not many people could read or write. Those who could were given very important jobs. Kings usually had a number of these workers, called scribes, write down important information about the kingdom. Scribes wrote down how much money the king paid or how much was owed by others. They wrote down a history of the kingdom's battles and wars."

Stefanie spoke up. "So King Saul's scribes wrote about the battle between David and Goliath."

"Right. And those records were kept as long as

there was a kingdom of Israel. In fact, all the stories about kings and wars in the Bible were probably written down first by a scribe."

"OK," I said. "Since there was someone whose job it was to write things down, the facts were probably written down right the first time. But what happened when those writings were copied by someone else?"

Mrs. Tipton reached for a piece of paper. "Keep in mind that they weren't writing these things down on paper like this. They were scratching their ink onto papyrus (pah-pie-russ) or parchment."

"That's right," I said. "Remember, Stef? We heard about that on our trip. Papyrus is made by beating reed plants flat, and parchment is made from dried sheepskins."

"Then you know that they worked out a way to make long rolls of the parchment," Mrs. Tipton said. "And the Israelites began to keep all their writings on these scrolls—the books of Moses, with all the stories in Genesis, and all the records of the kings and prophets. But the scrolls didn't last for very many years. So scribes also worked carefully to make copies of their writings onto new scrolls."

"And that's where the mistakes came in," I decided.

Mrs. Tipton nodded. "That's what you would think, isn't it? But the Hebrew scribes had a tradition of being very careful. A scribe would read the sentence he was about to copy, then read it out loud, and then write the sentence. When the scribe finished copying a whole book, he would count all the words in the original scroll, then count the ones in his copy to make sure they were the same."

"Wow," I said. "And I think I'm being careful when I check my spelling words twice."

"Not many years ago," Mrs. Tipton continued, "people were asking the same questions you are, Zack. They were sure there must be many mistakes in our Bibles because of all that copying. Then something remarkable happened."

Just then, something remarkable did happen. Rangoon jumped right out from behind a cabinet onto Stefanie's lap! "Aaah! Rangoon! You scared me!"

Rangoon just purred like a dump truck.

Mrs. Tipton laughed. "So he was hiding in here the whole time."

I tried to ignore the furry beast. "So what remarkable thing happened?" I asked.

"Well, the Hebrew scribes also had a habit of destroying all the old scrolls when new copies were made. So the oldest copies of the Old Testament books were copies made about 1,000 years after the time Jesus was on earth."

"That was a long time ago," Stefanie pointed out as she stroked the purring machine.

"Yes," Mrs. Tipton agreed, "but most of the books on those copies were written for the first time thousands of years earlier. Anyway, a boy herding goats near the Dead Sea threw a rock into a cave he saw and heard it break something. When he climbed into the cave, he found old clay jars filled with old scrolls."

I had heard that story before too. "They're called the Dead Sea Scrolls."

"Right you are, Zack," she agreed. "And people like myself discovered they were copies of Old Testament books a thousand years older than any other ever seen."

I snapped my fingers. "Now that would be a test. If the scribes were making mistakes in all their copies, then after a thousand years there would be a lot of changes in those books."

"That's what everyone said," Mrs. Tipton agreed. "But when they checked it out, they found that there were not many changes at all. Only a very few small mistakes were made."

I let out a big sigh. "Well, that's a big clue to this

mystery. Maybe we *can* believe that what's in our Bibles today is very close to what the first scribes wrote."

Mrs. Tipton smiled at me. "It's one of my favorite clues. Good luck finding more."

Just then, Rangoon leapt off Stefanie's lap and raced out the door. "Here we go again," Stef shouted. I followed her to the door, then turned back to Mrs. Tipton.

"Thanks," I said.

She was still smiling. "Good luck finding the cat too."

Clues About the Bible

Most of the stories in the Old Testament were probably written down by a king's or a prophet's scribes.

The writings and stories of the Israelites were collected onto scrolls by these scribes. Scrolls didn't last for many years, so new copies were made regularly. The Israelite scribes had a tradition of being very careful copiers.

For many years, the oldest copies of scrolls were made about 1,000 years after the time Jesus was here. The Dead Sea Scrolls were a thousand years older, and very few copying mistakes were found.

This is a really big clue that says we can believe the Bible stories of the Old Testament are a record of what really happened.

Words to Remember

Scribes: People who could read and write who were hired by kings and prophets to write down important things.

Papyrus: Writing tablet made by beating reed plants flat.

Parchment: Writing tablets made from dried sheepskins.

Scrolls: Long rolls of parchment.

CHAPTER ELEVEN

Trapped in Darkmoor Manor

This time, Rangoon hid in the women's W.C. We didn't find him until the screaming started. But before long, Stefanie had him out and we headed toward the front door. Stef thought it was funny. "I don't know why they screamed. Rangoon just likes people."

We almost ran into Charles on the stairs. He took one look at the cat and jumped back. "What is he doing here?" Charles demanded.

"Rangoon just wandered in," I answered. "We're taking him out." Charles took another look and hurried away. We walked on. "For a minute there, I thought he was going to scream too," I said. "He really doesn't like cats."

DETECTIVE ZACK

We spent most of the afternoon chasing the cat out. Luckily, Rangoon did take a nap for a while. Stefanie's mom stopped by and took us to something called "tea." Let me tell you something: If you like pretty flowers, pretty dresses, tea-that's-too-hot in pretty little cups sitting on pretty plates, be there. If you don't: Be somewhere else.

The little muffins were pretty good though.

When we got back, Mom was waiting by the car.. "I just wanted to see you before I left," she said. "Have fun at the soccer game." She hugged me then stopped to talk to Mrs. Townsend. "I'm sure they'll have a good time," she said. "And that they'll behave themselves."

"I'm not worried about it at all," Mrs. Townsend replied. "You enjoy yourself too."

"I will," Mom promised. "I'll be back," she called to me with a wave. Then she was gone.

By then, it was nearly closing time. "I saw that cat again," Mr. Townsend said when we walked in. "Let's be sure he's out of here before we close."

"Right, Father," Stefanie said. "Let's go, Zack." We patrolled the halls, asking everyone we met if they had seen a big yellow pain-in-the-neck. Finally, we tracked him down to a storage room near the W.C.

"Come here, Rangoon," Stefanie called. "Come

out from wherever you are under all the stuff."

Nothing happened.

"Here, Rangoony, goony, goony," I called. "Come out where we can find you." Nothing moved. "Are you sure he's in here?" I asked.

She was sure. "He has to be. The tour group that saw him go in here shut the door behind him. Push the door shut behind us so he can't escape."

I closed the door, and we spent a long time poking under crates and turning over boxes. Finally, we collapsed onto an old couch. "I give up," Stefanie said. Then, before she could say another word, Rangoon leapt down from a shelf over our heads right into her lap.

"Aaah! Rangoon, I'm going to choke you."

I wanted to choke him when Stef was finished. But I had to laugh. "He sat right up there and watched us the whole time. He was just waiting for us to give up. Come on, let's go."

But before we even got off the couch, the lights went out. "Hey," Stef cried out, "I can't see a thing in here."

I saw a sliver of light I hoped was from the door. "Stay still. I'll go open the door." After only one whack on the knee and a knocked over box, I pulled the door open. That let in more light, and Stefanie carried the cat out.

"Hey," she said when she got out in the hall-way, "Why is it so dark out here?"

I glanced out a window. "Well, for one thing, it's raining. There must a storm or something—the trees are really being blown around. For another thing, I think all the lights are out."

"You're right," she agreed. "Father must be getting ready to close. Let's hurry." We rushed to the office, but it was empty. "Where did everyone go?" Stefanie wondered. "Father! Hello! Is anyone here?"

While she was calling, I went to the front door. "Stef, stop," I said. "There's no one here. The door is locked."

"It can't be," she said, coming to try it herself. Of course, it didn't open. "But Father wouldn't . . ." She stopped, and her eyes got big. "Zack, did you tell your mother that you were staying with us tonight?"

"Of course," I answered. "I have all my stuff in my backpack in the office."

Stef dropped Rangoon and put her head in her hands. "My stuff is in the office too. I told my parents that I was going with you!"

It only took a few seconds for me to figure out that we were in trouble. "So neither one of them is going to miss us. No one is going to look for us."

"Wait!" Stefanie jumped up. "The alarm! It should go off any second now!" She jumped up and down and waved her arms. "Then the police will come, and we can explain what happened."

I just stood and watched her. Finally, she stopped. "The alarm isn't working if the electricity isn't working, is it?"

"It would have already gone off if it was going to," I agreed. "But what about the phone? Couldn't we call your parents?"

She was running toward the phone at the ticket desk before I finished my question. But the long wail that came next told me that the phones weren't working either. "That's it, then," I said. "We're trapped. In Darkmoor Manor."

Stefanie wasn't ready to give up. She went to the closest window and pushed back the glass. "Help!" she shouted. But the only thing in the parking lot was rain. "No one will hear us unless they drive up to the door." Then she shivered. "It's getting dark fast out there. We'd better find a torch quick."

"I know just where to get one," I told her. There was just enough light left for me to trot down the steps to the end of the hall. Then I stepped up onto the bench under the window and carefully lifted the torch from its holder. "Got it!" I called, and a few seconds later, I handed it to her.

Stef was almost mad. "Zack! Not that kind of torch! I meant the kind with batteries."

I scratched my head. "You mean a flashlight?" She nodded. "Well, why didn't you say so! This is no time to start speaking English."

"Well, let's hold onto this one," she decided. "And look for matches in case we don't find a real torch. I'll look in the office. You look behind the counter in the gift shop."

The only thing Stef found was that the office door was locked. I found the flashlight in the last place I looked—the top shelf under the counter. Of course, it was the last place I looked. Why would I keep looking after I found it?

"Stef!" I clicked the button on the big red flashlight—excuse me—"torch." The bright beam shone right in her face. "I found one."

She covered her eyes with her hand. "Oh, good. I really didn't want to be here all night in the dark. Now, please get that light out of my eyes."

After that, it got dark fast. We wanted to make the battery last as long as possible, so we shut off the light and sat down on the floor by the door. Rangoon disappeared into the darkness. "I guess there's not much hope that George will come back and check on the museum tonight," I finally said.

"Not after we trapped him last time," she agreed. "You don't think someone trapped us here on purpose, do you?"

I shook my head even though she couldn't see me. "No, we trapped ourselves. But don't worry. The electricity could come back on any minute. And when it does, alarms will be ringing all over the place."

"So will my parent's phone," Stefanie added. But she was a little worried. "You don't think that whatever happened to Ms. Huffington will happen to us, do you?"

CHAPTER TWELVE

Click, Clack, Clunk

I thought for a second. "If we really don't believe that she took the coins and left, then we have to believe that someone came in here with her."

"Or maybe after her, if she didn't lock the door or something," Stefanie guessed. "I still think someone was coming in at night, like she said."

I clicked on the light and stood up. "Maybe so. And since the only place someone could get in is through this door, we should think about waiting somewhere else."

Stefanie hopped up too. "You're right. Let's find another spot." She snapped her fingers. "I know! We'll go down and wait in Murphey's cell.

That's the last place anyone would go if they came in."

We walked slowly down the stairs. Outside, the wind was really howling. Stefanie shivered and rubbed her arms. "I'm glad I don't really believe in ghosts." Then she screamed.

"Aaah! Something hit me!"

I swung the flashlight around so fast I almost hit myself. But there was nothing in sight. Then I heard a rumbling sound. "Either someone just drove up out front in a tank or Rangoon is back."

As soon as he heard his name, Rangoon came prancing out from behind a display case. Stefanie tried to grab him, but he darted back and swatted a round, red rubber ball toward us.

Stefanie bent down and grabbed it. "Now, where did he find this?"

"Some kid probably lost it," I decided. Then I snatched it out of her hand. "Come on, let's play soccer in the hallway."

"Football," she reminded me. "OK, but put the light on the bench at the end. If I kick it past you to the wall, I score a goal. If you kick it past me, you score one."

"OK," I agreed. I set the flashlight down to shine across the floor and dropped the ball. The first one to get to it was Rangoon. He swatted toward my wall. "Hey, whose side are you on, anyway?"

We played for a while with Rangoon in the middle, racing after every kick and swatting it whenever he could. Finally, Stefanie stepped up on the bench and pushed the glass window open. "I'm hot," she said as she plopped down by the flashlight. "And hungry."

"Wait a second," I said as I reached into my jacket pocket. "I have two of those little muffins from the tea party. They are a little flatter than they used to be, but here, have them."

"Zack! You're not supposed to take muffins with you from tea." She grabbed them anyway. "But I'm glad you did. Thanks."

I reached down and snatched the ball away from Rangoon again. "So, you're a soccer—I mean football—playing cat. But are you any good at basketball?" I dribbled the little ball around Rangoon and looked for something to shoot at.

"Don't let him drool on you," Stefanie called to the cat.

I turned to make a face at her and saw the perfect basket—the torch holder by the window. With the torch out, it looked like a little basketball hoop. I was just taking a shot when it hit me. No, not the cat—a thought. I froze, and the ball bounced past me down the hall with Rangoon right behind.

"Zack, are you OK?" Stefanie asked.

I was thinking. *Round, like a basketball hoop.* "Stef, where are Murphey's three clues?"

She gave me a strange look. "Right there in his cell, over the table. Zack! Where are you going with that torch?"

I had grabbed the light while she was still talking. By the time she caught up, I was mumbling to myself. "It can't be this simple, can it?"

Stefanie thought I was crazy. "What can't be? Zack, we're not going to find Magic Murphey's secret way out. Just forget it."

I wasn't listening to her. "Remember when we looked at these clues before? I said that the flat circle looked like a basketball hoop. The first two clues look like the instructions to my adjustable basketball goal at home. When you want to make the hoop lower, you have to push the goal up first. That moves the lever so the goal can go down, just like the second clue. But in the third clue, the arrow goes to the right. What if . . ." I turned and headed back to the window and the torch holder.

Stefanie just watched while I hopped up on the bench. "It does look like a little basketball hoop," I decided. Then I reached over and pushed the hoop up.

It moved. *Click!*

Then I pulled down. It moved down lower than it was before I started. *Clack!*

I took a deep breath and twisted it to the right. *Clunk!*

Right beside me, the window bar closest to the torch dropped down halfway into the stone. That left a space big enough for a person to crawl through.

Stefanie sounded like she could hardly breathe. "That's it! Magic Murphey's secret way out! Zack, you found it! Wait until Father hears about this."

I was pretty amazed myself. "No wonder no one ever found it before. They weren't trying to play basketball."

Suddenly, Stefanie grabbed me. "Zack, we can get out! Come on, let's go find a phone and ring Father."

"Wait," I said. "Let's figure out how to get the bar back in place." I reached over and turned the torch holder back upright. Stefanie grabbed my arm.

"Not until we're outside," she demanded. "Here, help me get through."

I boosted her up, and she crawled out. Then I handed her the light, and I climbed out after her.

"The rain has almost stopped," she said, "but be careful by that muddy spot."

"I want to see if I can put that bar back in place," I said. "Hold the light for me." I bent down, grabbed the bar with both hands, and pulled. It was heavy but loose. I lifted it all the way into its hole in the top stone and heard a *click*. I let go, and it stayed in place. "Look at that," I said, pushing and pulling on the bar. "It's like it never moved."

Just then, Rangoon jumped right up in my face. I almost fell in the mud.

"Rangoon!" Stef reached over to grab him, but pulled back. "Now your feet are all muddy. Why don't you stay here and wait for us to come back."

I tried to herd him back through the window. He walked through the bars easily, but he wouldn't jump down to the floor. "Just push him," Stef said. "Then pull the glass window shut so he won't follow us."

As I gave him a shove, the light showed his muddy footprints all over the window sill. *I've seen those before*, I thought. Then something else clicked. Something important.

"Come on," I said as I jumped up. "Let's go call your father. I think I know how we can solve this whole mystery."

CHAPTER THIRTEEN

The Duke of Marbury

"I still don't know why I needed to make such a fuss about that title to the old Marbury estate today," Mr. Townsend whispered again.

Inspector Brown folded his arms. "I think the boy had a good idea. Besides, we'll know soon enough."

Stef looked at me and shrugged her shoulders. We were back in Magic Murphey's cell for the second night in a row. This time, we had to listen to an argument in whispers.

"Playing football was more fun," Stefanie whispered.

I agreed. "But at least this time, we're not trapped."

DETECTIVE ZACK

I had a hard time convincing Mr. Townsend to go along with my idea and set up another trap. "Find the title to the Marbury Estate and make sure everyone knows that you're asking Mrs. Tipton to come by and see if it's the original," I said.

"But she won't be able to tell," he protested. "She doesn't know anything about land titles."

I'm glad Inspector Brown was there. "It doesn't matter," he said. "If someone has been coming in here at night using Magic Murphey's window, then that person may be very interested in Marbury. Remember, Murphey was the Duke of Marbury."

For a while, I didn't think Mrs. Townsend was going to let Stefanie and me come back to Darkmoor with them. "Why, you two barely escaped that dreadful place just last night! You can't go back!"

But finally, we convinced everyone, and so there we sat, waiting. "I don't think anyone else has ever figured out Murphey's clues. So how could they come in this way? And why do we think this person will come tonight?"

Just then, there was a flash of light outside the window. The inspector snapped his torch off. "Silence," he hissed.

I could see the light in the window again, and then I heard the sound of the glass sliding back. I could barely see an arm-shaped shadow reach through around the window and grab the torch. Instead of taking the torch out first like I had, the hand lifted the torch and its holder.

Click. Clack. Clunk.

A few seconds later, a person wearing a black mask dropped to the floor. In an instant, Inspector Brown stepped into the hallway and clicked on his light. "No hurry," he said. "The alarm is already off."

With arms up to shield off the light, the person in the mask backed into the wall with a question: "What are you doing here?"

Inspector Brown kept the light on. "The question is, what are you doing here?"

Finally, I was sure. I jumped up to the cell door. "My question is, where is Ms. Huffington, Charles?"

Stefanie jumped up and stared at me. "Charles?"

Her dad was even more shocked. "Charles?"

The person in the mask slumped down onto the bench and pulled the mask off. It was Charles. "Good," he said quietly. "I'm glad it's over. Ms. Huffington is in my basement. And she's driving me loony!"

Inspector Brown pulled out a two-way radio and spoke to someone. Meanwhile, Stefanie had questions for me. "How did you know it was Charles?"

"Rangoon helped me figure it out," I told her. "Or at least, his big paw prints did. When I saw them on the windowsill last night, I knew I had seen them before. On Inspector Brown's car when we went to Ms. Huffington's house—and on Charles's car the morning Ms. Huffington disappeared. And remember, he told Inspector Brown that he had never been to Ms. Huffington's house. Then yesterday, when we almost bumped into Charles on the stairs, he saw Rangoon and said, 'What is he doing here?' How did Charles know it was a male cat? And remember how he jumped back? He's not afraid of cats. He recognized Rangoon. And Rangoon was supposed to be with Ms. Huffington."

Charles spoke up. "That blasted cat. She insisted that he had to be with her. After she caught me here and I had to lock her in my basement, I had to go and get her cat. I was trying to be nice!" he added to Inspector Brown.

"And that's when Rangoon walked on his car," Stefanie finished.

"That blasted cat," Charles repeated. "It ran

116

off and showed up here, of all places. I should have left it at the airport with her car."

Inspector Brown put away his radio and pulled out a notebook. "Did you also take the coins?" he asked.

Charles nodded. "Everyone should have blamed her for stealing them. But you two just wouldn't believe it, would you?" he glared at Stef and me.

Inspector Brown walked over to stand in front of him. "Charles, please state your full name."

Charles sighed. "Charles Edwin Murphey."

"Murphey! I should have known that." Mr. Townsend walked out by Inspector Brown. "That's why you know so much about Darkmoor. And that's what you've been looking for all these nights—the title to Marbury."

Charles lifted his head proudly. "That's right. My grandfather helped build this place. He was an expert with metal and gears. He never did trust the crown though. He knew they were out to get his estate. That's why he built in the escape— just in case."

Inspector Brown was busy writing. "So you have been entering Darkmoor at night to search for the Marbury title?"

"Of course I have," Charles replied. "Why do you think I took this job anyway? When I snatched a copy of the office door key so I could turn off that blasted alarm, I was set. I knew that title was here, and I knew that if I could get my hands on it, I would finally become the Duke of Marbury, as I should be." He was quiet for a moment; then, "How did you know about this window? No one knows this secret but the Duke of Marbury!"

Stefanie rolled her eyes. He was starting to sound a little loony to me too. But I answered him. "I guess it was just a lucky shot in the dark."

Anyway, that's all over now, and I'm on a train to Scotland with Mom. Scotland is part of the same country as England—it's all called Great Britain. I guess she found her old relatives up there, so we're going to see them. And get this: They live in a real castle!

Oh yes. Stefanie is going with us. When she heard about the castle, she was dying to go, and Mom was happy to invite her.

Ms. Huffington is fine. I guess Charles was very nice to her, except for keeping her locked in the basement—with the stolen coins. She says she talked to him all the time about turning himself in and getting some help with his problems.

Inspector Brown says that Charles is in jail, but he's being checked by some doctors. To me, he said, "Good job, Inspector Zack. I'll be in touch the next time I have a tough case."

When I talked to Dad on the phone last night, I told him all about Darkmoor. "Good thinking," he said. "I'm glad the tape recorder helped—even if that trap didn't work! I'm proud of you, Son."

I hurried on to tell him everything I had learned about the Bible, before he got too gushy. "Those are great clues," he agreed. "But let me tell you my favorite. Do you have your Bible there?"

I pulled it out of my suitcase. "OK. Now what?"

"Start with Luke 4:16. What does it say?"

I read it quickly. "It says that Jesus was in Nazareth, where he grew up, and that He went to church on Sabbath like He always did." I kept reading. "And I guess it was His turn to read the Scripture, so He read two verses from Isaiah about how God was sending someone to help the poor, to heal those who were hurt, and to set people free."

"Right," Dad said. "So Jesus picked up His Bible—our Old Testament, because the New Testament hadn't happened yet—and read those verses. Then what did He do?"

I read more. "It says He closed the book and sat down and that everyone was staring at Him. Then He told them, 'Today, these verses are coming true.' I guess He was saying, 'I'm the person God has sent to do these things.' "

Dad said, "So, do you think Jesus believed that the words spoken by Isaiah, the prophet, probably written down by a scribe, then copied over and over for hundreds of years, were still a true message from God?"

That was simple. "Of course He did. He knew that Isaiah was talking about Him." I thought for a second. "So if Jesus believed that the stories and writings in the Old Testament were still God's true messages, then I can too. You're right, Dad. That's the best clue of all."

Dad chuckled. "I don't think you've answered all the questions though. Since Jesus was here, the Old Testament and New Testament books have been copied again—this time into different languages. How do you know that the words Jesus spoke in the Hebrew, Greek, or Aramaic language are the same as what you read in English?"

I groaned. "I've found out that I don't even know some words they speak in English—at least not the kind of English they speak here. OK, that'll be the next big mystery. And this time, there won't be any Darkmoor mysteries to bother me."

This will just be a simple trip to an old castle.

At least, I hope it is.

I think.

Clues About the Bible

Since Jesus believed that the stories and writings in the Old Testament were still God's true messages, then I can too. That's the best clue of all.

Darkmoor Manor Mystery

Ms. Huffington is safely home with Rangoon. That makes Stefanie happy—and Mr. Townsend.

Who would have thought that basketball would help solve a mystery in England?

Words to Remember

Torch: A flashlight, in America.

Tea: Something to stay away from unless you like pretty little cups and things. Or good muffins.

And now,

FOR YOUR EYES ONLY,

a sneak preview

of

Detective Zack #10

THE SECRET OF
BLACKLOCH CASTLE

Coming soon!

CHAPTER ONE

Double Trouble

My pencil looks like it's at the end of a long math test—it needs to be sharpened, and the eraser is half gone. But I'm not doing math. In fact, I've decided that my math book was wrong. Sometimes, $1 + 1 =$ more than 2. I don't know how it does, but believe me—it does.

I'll start at the beginning. When my mom got the chance to go to a big meeting in England, she made plans to spent an extra week in Scotland to find some of her grandmother's relatives. I guess some of Mom's family came from Scotland to America many years ago.

My great-great-aunt and uncle live in a real, honest-to-goodness castle. It has towers, winding stairways, a dungeon, an empty moat, and secret passageways—at least that's what I've heard. It's called Blackloch Castle, and it has belonged to Mom's family for hundreds of years.

That's the good part. The bad part is, someone is trying to take it away from them—maybe. At least, that's what Uncle Ian (ee-un) says.

By the way, people from Scotland speak English a little differently than people from England or America. They often skip the "h" sound at the beginning of words. So "hard" is spoken like "ard." And "have" sounds like "ave." It's the same word, just with the "h" sound missing. Also, the "t" sound at the end of words is often left off. So "don't" becomes "don." It's spoken the same way, only without the "t" sound.

Anyway, Uncle Ian said, "We're trying 'ard to keep up with the old place. But the truth is, we're don' 'ave enough money or time to get it all done. The place is falling apart, I'm afraid."

Aunt Mary agreed. "I don' mind losing the old place so much—it's 'ard work to keep it up. But I 'ate for that Mr. MacTavish to gobble it up like a vulture. He's just waiting to plow it over and build 'ouses—mark my words."

"I wish we could find a way to help them," I told Mom later. "No one should bulldoze over a castle."

DETECTIVE ZACK

She seemed to be a little sad about it too. "We can't give them enough money to make a real difference. It would take a fortune to repair this place."

I could only come up with one idea—and it was pretty lame. "What we need to do is find a buried treasure. That would save their castle."

Mom laughed. "Did I tell you? There's a treasure map over the fireplace. They found it a long time ago, and it's been hung up there like a painting for ages. No one believes the treasure exists anymore though."

A treasure map!

An old castle!

"Stef," I said when I found her in her room, "I think I have a plan."

Stef wasn't happy. "I hope it includes filling that moat up with water again and throwing those two into it." She pointed out the window at two boys who seemed to be working on a machine that would throw things a long distance—like all the way up to her window.

I stuck my head out to get a closer look. And you have to look close to see any differences between the two. Edwin and Edgar are Aunt Mary's identical twin eight-year-old great-grandsons. Lucky for us, they're visiting at the same time we are. "They've been practicing with water balloons. But it looks like they have some big fruit now."

Stefanie leapt up and snatched the windows closed, almost knocking me over. "Hey, don't get mad at me," I said.

She just glared. "They're your cousins."

"I think they're my fourth cousins, twelve times removed."

Stefanie raised one eyebrow. "Well, I don't know what "fourth cousins" means, but I can sure understand why they keep getting removed."

This definitely was going to be an interesting week.